Good Night, God Bless

Susan Heyboer O'Keefe

Illustrated by Hideko Takahashi

Henry Holt and Company

New York

Henry Holt and Company, LLC, *Publishers since 1866*
115 West 18th Street, New York, New York 10011

Henry Holt is a registered trademark of Henry Holt and Company, LLC

Published in Canada by Fitzhenry & Whiteside Ltd.,
195 Allstate Parkway, Markham, Ontario L3R 4T8.

Library of Congress Cataloging-in-Publication Data
O'Keefe, Susan Heyboer.
Good night, God bless / Susan Heyboer O'Keefe; illustrated by Hideko Takahashi.
Summary: A child's good-night prayer, encompassing familiar objects and people.
1. Children—Prayer books and devotions—English. [1. Prayers.]
I. Takahashi, Hideko, ill. II. Title.
BV265.044 1999 242'.82—dc21 98-42724

ISBN 0-8050-6008-1 / First Edition—1999
The artist used acrylic on illustration board to create the illustrations for this book.
Typography by Martha Rago
Printed in Italy
10 9 8 7 6 5 4 3 2

For my parents with love

—S. H. O'K.

To Tatsuo and Mitsuyo

—H. T.

Good night, God bless
Our world at rest,
Each hillside dark
And evening dressed.

The moon
A silver coin mid-air,
The forest black
As coal laid bare.

Good night, God bless
All creatures' sleep,
The air now hushed
Of growl and peep.

Each bear cub dozing
In its den,

Each yearling hidden
In the glen.

Each sparrow silent
In its nest,
Each gentle lamb
At mother's breast.

Good night, God bless
Our town at rest,
Which counts each person
As a guest.

The school that's waiting
To be filled,

The church's choir
Of voices stilled.

The empty roads
That long for cars,
The darkened windows
Filled with stars.

Good night, God bless
Our home at rest,
Its every room
A treasure chest.

Instead of gold
There is a ball
And photos hanging
On the wall.

An open book,
Two shoes untied,
Four toothbrushes
Set side by side.

Good night, God bless
Our family's rest.
Bless everyone
Whom we love best.

Bless those we live with
Every day.
Bless those who must be
Far away.

And bless me, too,
And please say yes
To this, my prayer—
Good night, God bless.